WORRY!

Michael Buxton

Kane Miller
A DIVISION OF EDC PUBLISHING

Deep down in the coral reef, lived a puffer fish called Peter.

Peter worried a lot.
And when he worried,
he puffed up into
a big ball.

Peter worried
about new things.

But his friends
helped him feel better.

Peter worried about having bad dreams.

But Ollie said sometimes dreams were fun.

Peter worried about going to the dentist.

But Greg said the dentist helped keep his smile healthy.

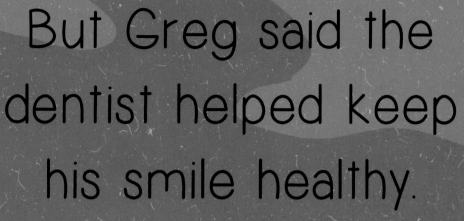

Peter worried
about the dark.

But Dottie showed Peter all the wonderful things to see at night.

Peter wasn't the only one worried about the first day of school.

But together ...
they had lots
of fun.